MW01047375

# Like Sunshine On an Otherwise Miserable Day

By Kelly M. Byrd

Illustrated by Patricia Vásquez de Velasco

Byrdhouse
PUBLISHING

Copyright © 2019 Kelly M. Byrd.

All rights reserved. This book or any portion thereof may not be reproduced or used in any manner whatsoever without the expressed written permission of the publisher except for the use of brief quotations in a book review.

Printed in the United States of America.
Library of Congress Cataloging-Publication Data is available

Second Edition, 2019.

ByrdHouse Publishing, LLC
P.O. Box 27803
Saint Louis, MO 63146-9998

ISBN: 978-0-578-57781-4

This book is dedicated to **Patricia C. McKissack**.

Thank you for our sweet tea conversations. Thank for your love, your wisdom, your breadth of work, and your willingness to share. But most of all, thank you for being the "sunshine" for a girl who wanted to write.

I just LOVE sunshine!

I love how it streaks through my windows and brightens my room and how the sun dances on my skin and warms me from the inside out. But what I love most of all are the fun things I can do outside in the sun, like swimming, playing tag with my friends, and hula hooping!

Do you know how to make sunshine?

Well I do, and I bet you can, too!
Let me tell you a story about how I made
sunshine on an otherwise miserable day.

I woke up early in the morning. I was super excited thinking about all the fun my doll Luna and I were going to have outside in the sun.

But when I looked out
the window, it was raining
cats and dogs!
There was no sunshine
at all.
I knew it was going to be
a miserable day.

I pouted my way to the kitchen.

"Mom, I thought I was going to have fun outside, but it's raining, so the sun can't shine!".

"You can make your own sunshine, Kanilou," Mom said.

"How can I make sunshine?"

"Well, since you can't be happy doing your outdoor activities, you have to find a way to be happy doing your indoor activities instead. That's what I do.

Let's start right now.
How about you come give me a big warm hug."

I grabbed my favorite funny book.
"Beau, would you like me to read to you?"
"Yeah, yeah, yeah!" he said with a smile. When Beau giggled,
his little tummy wiggled. He laughed so hard that he knocked over his blocks.

I could feel the sun bursting from the inside out.
It felt so good it made me want to shout.
Creating sunshine in my own way,

Doing fun things with my family, when I
couldn't go out and play, felt like sunshine
on an otherwise miserable day.

I found my big brother Baxter drawing in his room. Baxter is a great artist! I pulled a chair right up next to him so I could draw, too. I watched Baxter very closely to learn how I could make my picture just right!

"Your drawing is pretty good, Lou!" That put a smile on my face.

I could feel the sun bursting from the inside out.
It felt so good it made me want to shout.
Creating sunshine in my own way,

Doing fun things with my family, when I
couldn't go out and play, felt like sunshine
on an otherwise miserable day.

I went to show Dad my picture.

"It's a masterpiece, Kanilou! Come have a seat. I've got a story to share about me and you."

My Dad told me how he liked to draw pictures when he was a little boy. Guess what — he liked to draw horses, just like me!

I could feel the sun bursting from the inside out.
It felt so good it made me want to shout.
Creating sunshine in my own way,

Doing fun things with my family, when I
couldn't go out and play, felt like sunshine
on an otherwise miserable day.

In the kitchen, my Mom had out a loaf of bread, peanut butter, bananas, and honey.

"Mom, peanut butter and banana sandwiches are my favorite. And Luna's, too!"

"I know," Mom said. "And we are going to make this one extra special, sweet girl, just for YOU."

I drizzled that golden yumminess
ALL over the bananas and peanut butter.
The honey looked like a stream of sunshine.
Then I smashed the two slices of bread
together. I couldn't wait to take a bite!

I could feel the sun bursting from the inside out.
It felt so good it made me want to shout.
Creating sunshine in my own way,

Doing fun things with my family, when I
couldn't go out and play, felt like sunshine
on an otherwise miserable day.

By the time I finished my delicious snack, the sun was shining bright, and the whole family went outside to enjoy the

BEAUTIFUL SUNSHINE!

I learned that when you have fun with others, you feel happy, and they do, too. YOU can make your own sunshine anytime you want.

Even on an otherwise miserable day.

The End

List 10 things that you can do to
"make your own sunshine".

1.

2.

3.

4.

5.

6.

7.

8.

9.

10.

Made in the USA
Middletown, DE
08 November 2024

63979386R00018